MYA

MYA

Oppression to Progression for Black Women in the West Indian Slave Trade

—— by ——

SANDRA MADDIX

authorHOUSE®

AuthorHouse™ UK
1663 Liberty Drive
Bloomington, IN 47403 USA
www.authorhouse.co.uk
Phone: 0800.197.4150

Published by AuthorHouse 09/04/2015

ISBN: 978-1-5049-4327-7 (sc)
ISBN: 978-1-5049-4328-4 (e)

Print information available on the last page.

Any people depicted in stock imagery provided by Thinkstock are models,
and such images are being used for illustrative purposes only.
Certain stock imagery © Thinkstock.

This book is printed on acid-free paper.

INTRODUCTIONS. FORMALITIES, DEDICATIONS
AND THANKS

This entire book is a work of fact and non-fiction. The first part is non-fiction. A story, about a little girl and her mum born free and then enslaved. It is called Mya, The Story of a Slave Girl.

Although a work of fiction, it actually outlines actual events that would happen to a black woman in slavery during the period I am writing about in the 18th and 19th centuries, during the West Indian Slave Trade.

The second part is fact. It is based on factual events about the West Indian Slave Trade named, Oppression to Progression for Black Women in Slavery. I have utilised throughout my work using many references which will establish and authenticate that these experience actually happened.

I will mention these many writers/authors names and the content of their work/thoughts in relation to my own in creating this piece of work and eventually writing a book that I can prove of.

This is my own work which I submitted at the beginning of my career, but unfortunately at the time could not find the right publisher. I hope you find my book very interesting and educational .

These authors in their own right have written historical events concerning the slavery period of my book and they will show the conditions and validate my findings and substantiate my work by their own work.

Their names which I have had the privilege to mention and study in order to complete my book are Beckles' & Bush, Richardson, Bell Hook and Binder and Reimers'. I have also used other references and i hope you will find it helpful whilst reading my book with the understanding that this will is only the beginning and not the end for me in bringing historical events into your homes to become aware of and how it has affected the very lives we live today.

It is important for people to know their beginnings before they can set a future agenda for themselves and believe that anything is possible as long as they are determined an d are willing to overcome any hurdle that comes in their way. They will eventually succeed!

DEDICATION

This work I would like to dedicate to all of the young people out there who are trying to achieve something in their life and simultaneously give back something to society.

We all require some sort of start in life to play a big instrument in how and who we will become as an artiste or a person of value.

I would also like to say many thanks to my children Jurita and Ceake for giving me the inspiration to achieve my goals and ambitions and realise that it is never too late for me to continue my work even if it just for self but also to inspire others.

Love Sandra Maddix

1/ MYA The Story of a Slave Girl

2/ OPPRESSION TO PROGRESSION FOR BLACK
WOMEN IN SLAVERY

BY SANDRA MADDIX

Mya, was born of African heritage. She was a Princess amongst her people and her Mother a Queen of the Tribe. She did not do anything really. All she understood was that she was treated differently and always shown respect and adorned with the most fabulous clothing. She was happy and her Mother was always laughing, smiling and giving her kisses and hugs. She really loved her mum and wondered sometimes why she never saw her dad so much. But as per usual her mummy would always explain, 'He is a very important Man and has many things to do but he does love you'. This was enough for her. Anything her Mother said was enough and meaningful to her.

Mya played in the gardens and picked fresh fruit and vegetables to eat. She was a very happy child and had lots of attention.

Her mother told her she was of royalty, but she did not understand. Her Mother told her where she came from and that she was a Princess there too and had all of the lovely things that Mya had now and that she would always be protected and one day she would be Queen of their Village.

This pleased Mya greatly because mummy was smiling. Her Mother's smile was of pure sunshine and she was so beautiful.

Mya asked her in a little way why they were so different from the other people, but her mummy explained somewhat to her understanding, "We are not chile. It's just that mummy don't come from here. But where I come from the stars shine just as bright and the moon and the sun are still the same. My people are of not of your Father's people, dat all. But together we will make a change and unite our people as one".

Mya smiled and looked at her Mother and then asked her with a serious face, "Are you happy mummy? Her mother patted her on the back and with a deep sigh put her finger under Mya's chin and said, why do you ask me that? Of course I am. I do as my Father ask and I have you. Please don't be silly. These things are expected of women and their husband, much less their

Father and one day your time will come and you will have to do as he says".

Mya looked at her Mother and could see by the look in her eyes do not ask me any more questions. That was the last conversation they had until they were sent away.

Mya did not remember much, but she did remember her Mother and Father arguing and shouting at each other. She had never heard them speak to each other that way before. Then her Mother came out of the place with her hand on her face and said in a whisper, "We have to leave now. Do not take anything. They are waiting for us".

Before she could reply her mummy had walked away shaking her head and weeping. She had never seen her Mother cry before. She was tempted to enter her Father's home but during her hesitation he came out and shook his hands meaning be off with you. She looked at him not knowing it would be for the last time and walked away slowly towards her mother.

She can't really remember much after that. Perhaps it was all a blur, but she does remember they were on a boat, a big one with many people and it was rocking back and forth so much until she was sick.

Her Mother grabbed her and she turned around surprised to see and she asked her sobbing, "Mummy, why? Where are we going?"

Her Mother replied, "You ask too many questions. You are with me and I had to travel further than this. Hey look at me, I must admit the conditions were better, but we will survive, your Father promised me that. Don't give me that look now. It was for the Village. The safety of our people, otherwise they would have taken us all. You see chile. Don't worry and no more talking, just stay close to me and when we reach where we are going we will be together. Now go to sleep and rest in my arms, mummy is here and I will never leave you".

Her Mother rocked her back and forth in rhythm with the both ship and Mya slept comfortably in her mother's arms.

When she woke up her mummy was still holding her humming away as if they were going into the gardens. She rubbed her eyes and smiled at her and her mummy smiled back, stroking her beautiful hair that she could remember before they shaved it off.

All she could she think about was survival and why me and my baby. Why didn't he go and protect the village? Are we considered lesser than him? Without her wealth he would be nothing and at war, probably dead by now, but no. The easy way for him, he gave us away. Me, ok, but our chile, our beautiful, innocent chile. What God has he sent us to? What kind of a man is this? She shook her head deeply in shock because for the first time she realised they were slaves. He sold them to protect the Village but mainly the men. She felt disgusted at herself, but it was a lesson she would never forget.

Finally they were there, whatever there was. Mya could see from her Mother's face that she was afraid. She held her very tightly and bent over, not looking up. She could not understand. Then a man shouted out from the crowd, "Them two are mines. Paid and bought for, here are my documents. Now give them to me".

The man looked at the papers and took us to him. He looked at us and turned my mum around. Laughing aloud, smiling and saying aloud, "Royalty". He then took my Mother by the arm and led her to his carriage. To me he seemed nice even though for the first time I had seen so many people of this colour before. I was tempted to touch his skin to see if it was real.

He was speaking to my Mother in a tongue that I had never heard before and I could see that she kind of understood him, but did not like what she could understand. I would soon.

We arrived at one of the biggest places I had seen in my life. It was all white with big columns and a door able to fit four men from shoulder to shoulder to enter. To me it looked meaningless, but Mother smiled and turned to me saying, "This is our new home and we will always be together as I promised Mya".

She bent down on her knees and then said again, "remember I told you about the moon and stars, it's the same here too. But this man here is going to look after us now and no matter what we have to listen and obey his laws or we will be beaten. Do you understand me? Obey Mya and then we will live well."

I said to her, "Who is he? Why did they shave off my hair?" She did not answer, but looked down to the ground and when she lifted up her and saw my face she replied, "It was nothing, it will grow back even more beautiful than ever and you will one day rule all you can see and Mya you have to learn his language, we are not allowed to speak like this anymore. Do you understand, but at the same time never forget?"

I nodded, what else could I do and then I looked at the pot bellied man and realised he reminded of my father except for his colour.

I don't know where we went. But everyone was staring at us and especially this beautiful woman. Her hair was the colour of corn flowers and her skin was so white and she had on a dress that I had never seen before. It was the colour of her skin and made her look even whiter.

She smiled at me and beckoned me to come to her. I looked at my Mother. She pushed me forward to go to her and as I reached her not knowing what to do, I then again looked at my Mother. She looked at me and smiled and bowed and so I did the same to this strange Lady.

She put her hand on my face and ran over to the pot bellied man and kissed him and then ran back to me. She held me by the hand and literally pulled me along with her talking so fast. But it did not make a difference because I did not understand at all. She was happy. I don't know why, but I would soon.

I looked back at my Mother and she told me "Go on have some fun, remember what I said now. I love you and I will see you soon. Be good and do whatever they ask of you. Go on".

"Ok Mama, see you soon. I promise I will be good. Love you Mother". I ran with the Lady and when I turned around again my Mother was gone. I could not see her. I was afraid and stopped, pulling my hand from the Lady. She stopped and looked at me and realised I was afraid. She looked around and then pointed with her finger and said, "There. Look over there, Mama, there". I looked where she pointed and saw my Mother. She waved at me and even from that distance I could see her beautiful smile.

I looked at the Lady and smiled at her. My hands relaxed, I walked and then ran with her. I felt alright now. She can't be someone to be an afraid of and I had never seen anyone including my Mother kiss my Father like that or no one else for that matter. It was new but quite enlightening.

My life, my days went pretty quick after that. I learnt their language and I could write and also speak another language they called French. The Lady's name was Sarah and she was my best friend. We played together and I slept in the same room as her, only my bed was a lot smaller and not so grand. I wore beautiful clothes like her and as Mother promised my hair grew back even more beautiful than ever.

I saw my Mother quite often and sometimes she looked fat and then she was small again, but I still received a lot of kisses of hugs and she spoke just like me. Just like the white people and black people who I saw working all day. But it was no different to what I remember of being home.

I looked at the stars and the moon at night and they looked the same, but everything else looked different. I felt loved and Sarah was always there, so I never felt alone. I loved her and I knew she loved me.

I was fifteen by now and had my seeing of womanhood at thirteen. I was as everyone kept saying skinny. My skin had got lighter from their pale sun and my hair had got blacker like unburned coal. My eyes had also changed colour, but I had seen these changes in my Mother. She explained to me that it was due to their climate and that I was fortunate and looked like her people. That was good enough for me because my Mother was the most beautiful person I saw and everyone when I saw her walking around would be staring at her, as she walked on by with her head held up very high.

My Queen! She looked and always smelt good, like food. Sometimes she smelt so good I always wanted to eat after she left. I did not do anything else but give her all the time we were allowed to spend together. It was not long enough for me, but I could see her outside. It reminded me of home in a way and I did not miss my Dad until now.

That day changed my whole life all over again. Sarah's Dad called for me and she told me to go quickly as I would make him angry. I ran to him and knocked on the door, he called in, "Mya". I entered and curtsied, "Yes Sir".

He beckoned me forward and looked me up and down and then moved from around his desk and came towards me. He sort of grunted um uh and then put his hands on my bottom. Yes, beautiful, nice and firm. Then he said to me, "Mya, do you know why I called you?" I answered, "No Sir. I have done something to displease you Sir?" He replied, "On the contrary Mya, you have grown up to be the most desirable woman on this plantation and I, yes I, and intend to have you for myself. Do you understand what I am saying to you?"

He put his index finger under my chin and pulled my head up to his eyes. Grey they were and winkled. His skin was blemished from old age and he looked so old, but yes I knew exactly what he meant. I simply nodded.

It was quick and painful and I bled. He laid back on the chaise lounge and pointed to a chamber pot so I could wash myself. I did. I got dressed and looked at him, he was sleeping and just like that I quietly walked out of the room and shut the door.

I ran and ran, looking for Mother. Where was she? I saw here and ran over to her. Crying fitfully, panting, and my chest heaving I looked up to her, but before I could utter a word she said whilst stroking my head, "I knew this day would come. Soon you will be with chille. You are now massa's woman to do as he please. Why did you think he gave you such beautiful things and could not resist you?"

I looked at her, "Mama did he take you too?" She sighed and then answered me with what I realised for the first time a very tired face. Still beautiful and graceful, but very tired. "Yes, but I am too old now and he wants more babies. Now I know you don't want to hear me baby chile, but this is what we women are meant to do. Don't blame him. That's all any man wants from a woman, especially when they are as beautiful as you. But I am just plain tired now and I can't have no more babies and go telling anybody nothing. I am sure he will sort everything out when you get fat wid chile, just like me and then everything go back to normal. But you don't let somebody else touch you. You belong to him now, in every which way. You understand".

My Mother spoke to me in our language and it was hard to comprehend but then it came back to me. I was his wife, only I did not see any marriage. "Ok Mother. I am sorry. I understand"

She kissed me on my forehead and held me in her arms, like for the longest time ever and when she let go she put her arms on my shoulders and stared at me. I did not see that look before. It was, I don't know, different and then she kissed me and smiled and walked away never turning to look at me. I walked back to the house not quite sure what just happened, all I knew for certain was that my life was never going to be same again.

As I entered the house I crept passed his big doors and went up the stairs to Sarah's room. She was sitting on her bed and I knew she was pretending to read, as she hummed under her breath. "Well what Papa wanted of you? Are you in trouble for something, because I cannot think for the life of me, what it could be for?"

I looked at her, she knew. She knew but was too afraid for some reason. I answered her, "Nothing Miss Sarah, he just wanted to know about my well-being and if I was happy".

She quickly rose up her head and stared frightfully at me and then jumping out of her bed she said, "He said something else to you didn't him? He not is taking you away from me. Never! I, Just won't allow it? You are my slave, mines to keep. He promised".

Before I could answer her back, she looked at me and said, "You did tell him that didn't you Mya?"

"No Miss Sarah, he didn't ask about you or I in that way and he didn't really just asked if I was happy. I don't think he will take me away from you and I don't want to leave you, you are my best friend. I don't want to leave you or my Mother".

She grabbed me muttering and sighing and then said, "That's the truth?" I replied, knowing I was lying, but I knew it was for my own protection and that of my Mother and know I knew for certain what my Mother meant, so I answered her saying, "No, that was all. I don't things will change around here for a long time. Do you want to do anything special today? I want to make you happy. I don't like it when you are sad. It makes me sad too."

"No, not really, lets' just do what we always do". We smiled at each other and began to giggle like children, only I was no longer a child and the longer she did not know of what just happened the better things would be.

The Master of the house, Sarah's Papa would call upon me often but never to her knowledge. It was like our little secret, but I suspected that the housemaids knew of it, because they would always scrutinise me as I walked by and found that they did not like me at all. Their main focus upon me always seemed to my belly.

I told the Master of this and he made different arrangements for us to be together. I always felt dirty and would scrub my skin so much until something it felt dry and sore all over. But I could still smell him all over me. He really thought I enjoyed it and would take Sarah and me into town in the carriage and buy lots of beautiful of gowns.

I awoke one morning feeling really ill and could not stop being ill. Sarah called for the housemaid, who then must have told the Master. The doctor came and took me to another room and examined me and then told me I was with child and that everything would be fine and that soon the sickness would pass. He then left telling me to stay put.

A little later I saw my Mother, I was so happy to see her. But this time she did not cuddle or kiss me but just simply said, "Come on then, you are coming to stay with me until the baby is born. No one must know. Well get up then, we haven't got all day".

I got out of the bed slowly, holding onto my stomach, feeling like I was going to be ill again. She pointed her finger at me and said directly, "Not know, we have no time for that. Now get moving". I answered quietly, my throat feeling dry and sore, "Ok Mother". We left.

Where my Mother lived reminded me of home, but instead it made out of wood. She had a bed that looked more like a cot and rocking chair and a table with draws. On top of the table there was a lamp and a few trinkets that looked like they did not belong there. These must be gifts, because I had similar trinkets of the same fashion, but I was not allowed to show them to anyone. The Master would always tell me there were mines, put them on me when we were finished and then insist I take them off again and then he would put them in a special box and put them away.

My Mother, after what seemed like an eternity then turned to me and said, "I knew this day would come. I was only waiting. He must have called for you often for you to be with child so quick. Don't answer me, it does not matter. He will leave you alone now until the baby comes and then you can go back to the house, but for now you stay with me and in this house until that baby is born. Do you hear me?"

I nodded. I had so many things to ask her, but I could see this was not the right time. She pointed to the bed/cot and went and sat on the edge of it. I saw a chamber pot underneath it and another blanket folded neatly at the end. She had a curtain of sorts drawn across a little area in the house and next to that something that appeared to be a stove with pots and pans. Above it I could see some plates and cutlery and a few cups.

She then turned to me and came towards to me. I bent down my head. I did not know what she was going to do or say. "Mya, she said, as she bent down. Look at me. I am not angry with you. I am angry with him. He could have had anyone and he chose my only true child, born legal in wedlock. The only one I was allowed to keep as long as I did as I was expected and when he saw I could not have no longer have any more babies, he took you. For that I cannot forgive him. I do not envy you, but I curse your beauty because if you were ugly he would not have taken you.

It is my fault, not yours and the worse thing is that he will never leave you alone now and you will never see your children because he will take them from you. They are not yours but his to do with has he please".

She then stood up brushed down her skirt and walked out of the house. I was left there on my own for appeared to be hours before she came back.

When my Mother did finally come back she ushered me towards the area where the curtain was and pulled it back shoving me gently behind it before closing them and then I heard voices. I did not recognise them but my Mother was obviously instructing them on where to place to certain items and then she told them to leave. Then there was silence. I saw a dim light appear through the curtain and was going to come out when I heard her voice saying, "Not yet, stay there". I remained standing and then looked around the little area. It had loads of beautiful clothes like I had never seen my Mother worn before and when I touched them, they felt so soft and delicate. They were of all different colours. As I held one up to my face I saw shoes with heels. My Mother's, they had to be. I had to be, but I had never seen my Mother in heels before. I then I wondered where would she wear such beautiful clothes and things?

She then called me out. I looked at the house hardly recognising it. There was a new bed, curtains and another chair. She had various pots and pans. Basically, everything was new and it looked great. I did not care about being with child anymore. It was obvious Master had provided all of these things so that we could live in comfort.

I looked at her smiling and then she smiled back. She looked happy and then said to me, "tomorrow we had to leave here, but massa wanted you to be in comfort until then. I am to take care of you until your time comes and then you can go back to the house. But understand this Mya, under no circumstances are you to show your face to anyone else. You stay in here always, no matter what and always keep them curtains drawn"

"Ok Mother, I will. Where are we going tomorrow?" She replied, "Never you mind. Now get some sleep and I will make you some tea to settle your stomach. Well what are waiting for, take off those things and put this on and lay down, we don't want nothing going wrong with you or the child. You are all mines for now".

With that, she went to the stove and made the preparations. I got dressed in my night gown and went under the sheet and waited for her. I had so many things to ask her, but before I knew it I was fast asleep.

I woke up to hear my Mother singing a song that I had not heard since we left home. She used to sing it to me all of the time. I laid there listening to her gentle voice and watched her as she prepared our meal. It smelt delicious. She turned and looked at me and then came over to me with a cup of tea. It smelt horrible but she held it to my mouth all the same and made me sip it before passing the cup to me.

I took my time and eased myself up in the bed making sure as to not spill the tea and then drank it all. She then came to me and took the cup and looked into it and went, "Good chile, you are having a boy, Massa will be happy. When did you start not feeling yourself?"

I looked at her puzzled, quite taken back and then answered, "About two or three weeks ago, but I have not bled for nearly three, why and how you know it will be a boy?" She looked at me and laughed a little and then stroked my face, "An old custom, one that has been passed down from Mother to Mother by reading the residue of your tea, but it seems you to be too small for that long, but it does not matter we will just have to prepare a bit quicker, just in case it does comes as you say".

"But Mother, I don't understand what you are saying". She sigh heavily, one that blew out of her nostrils and then replied, "Their are many things you do not know Mya because you were not taught them. But if you look into the cup you will see it all". "See what Mother?" "Just look into the cup".

She passed it back to me and all I could see was wet tea leaves at the bottom. I said to her, "I see tea leaves that seem to be piled a little in the middle but there is no circle, but that's it". My Mother, then replied, "That means it will be a boy. If the leaves were round without a mount then it shows it will be a boy. That's good. It means Massa might keep him and he won't have to work in the fields. It all now depends on his looks. Looks are very important to Massa, Mya".

"But why Mother?" She answered, "Well if he too dark then it will determine how Massa will deal with him. He might sell him or keep him to work in the fields. If he comes out like us, then it is more likely that Massa will keep him and educate him to a certain level. But you must remember this if you ever see him, which I hope you don't, you are never and I mean never to recognise or acknowledge or you both will go. Do you understand me?"

I did not understand why and so I asked her. "Because the baby will belong to Massa not you. We were bought from your Father for that purpose, Mya. To have babies. We receive special treatment from like that of the other slaves because of this reason and no other, but if we break them then we will be separated. So we have to as we are told. Now I have told you all of this and I don't want to talk about it ever again?"

Now I understood, now I understood everything. I was going to be just like my Mother. I felt ashamed and I could not wait for this thing to come out of me because I would never be able to call him my son. For the longest I looked at my Mother, she turned her head away and when she looked back at me she bent forward and kissed me face saying, "My poor little Mya, you had no idea, but I did not have the courage to tell you. I was praying there would be no need for it" and then she began to cry a little before wiping away her tears and getting up. She walked back over to the stove and carried on cooking.

The next day very early in the morning we left my Mother's house. I wouldn't see it again. We rode for what seemed for ever until we came to a small little cottage. When we entered it was quite beautiful and we there was a maid and a manservant.

It appeared to have small luxuries and I was quite pleased with it. I had my own room for the first time in my entire life and a bed big enough for two people, but it still was a lot smaller than Sarah's. That was the first time I thought of Sarah since leaving the house.

I wondered if she knew and how she would treat me when I returned. So many things were racing through my head. I set them aside once my Mother entered my room. She looked at me and then said, "We will be comfortable here. Don't worry about a thing. You may go outside whilst we are here but not too far. If you need again just pull that cord. I will come and attend to you. No one else. Now unpack your things and make yourself comfortable. I will call you when breakfast is ready. Here is a cup of tea to settle your stomach, make sure you drink it whilst it is hot and I will come back for you soon".

She then turned and walked straight out of my room. I looked around my room again and flopped down on my bed. The only thing that I realised I was happy about was that I was going to be with my Mother and I intended to make the most of precious time together with her as much as possible. It was going to be much better than the little visits spared to me when I was in the house, as I did realise they were becoming fewer.

I put my things away quickly as there was not much and waited for her patiently as I drank my tea. She came back to me. She looked at me and looked at my room. She seemed pleased and then said, "Are you happy? I got up and approached her replying back, "Yes Mother, more than happy. I hope to spend all of my time with you and I can't wait to have this baby, but at the same time it saddens me to know that once I do I won't see as much as often. So I hope you will promise me now that we will spend each waking moment together as much as possible. The only request I have of you, please forgive me Mother is that you stay with me in my room with me please".

She smiled. Oh God she was so beautiful and then answered, "My you have grown up and if you wish my daughter of course I will. I will make the arrangements now and it should be done by the time we have done our meal. Now come with me and we eat and I will show you around and introduce to our servants". "Yes Mother and Mother, thank you". I then kissed her and we put our hands in one and walked down to passageway into the kitchen.

We ate a beautiful breakfast and then she introduced me to the servants and then showed me the grounds and the garden. It was quite beautiful and peaceful. I wished I could stay here forever. She then explained to me that if in the future I ever got pregnant again I would always come here and she would be the one to look after me.

In one way I hoped, how I hoped I would be pregnant all of the time just to be with my Mother but at the same time I thought of Master or massa as Mother called him touching me and doing those things. I didn't like it. I automatically took the thought out of my head and didn't think about it again until he turned up.

It was only a few days later. My Mother called me and when I went to her there he was standing, smiling away. He asked me how was I doing and if I was pleased with him and then he took my Mother away and spoke to her and then left.

I expected my Mother to say something but she did not. The time went so quick and then the pain began. It lasted for a few hours and I did have a beautiful baby boy. My Mother made me hold him for a few minutes and then took him away. I never saw him again. When she re-entered my room she came with the maidservant and helped me out of the bed. She washed me down and changed my gown and by the time she had finished and she drew back the curtains from my bed, everything was as nice and clean, as if I had not even slept in it. I soon enough fell straight back into a deep sleep.

We remained there for a further two months as I was quite poorly and kept bleeding. My Mother confined me to my bed and looked a little concerned, but as time went by I grew stronger and felt myself again.

Then they came for us. She explained it was time for me to go back to the house and that she would see as before. I never asked about the baby but just listened to her. She did not say much and so I did not ask her anything. I was sad and I could not even tell her but despite all of that she looked much better and I looked more beautiful, or so she kept telling me.

We went back to the house. As the carriage dropped her off she kissed me and smiled as per usual and walked away and then continued onto the house. It still looked the same. Nothing had changed. Master and Sarah were waiting for me on the porch. As I climbed the stairs she ran into my arms and then looked at me and said, "But Mya you looked absolutely radiant. I have never seen you look so fine. They told me you were sick, but obviously you are much better now. Please don't get ill like that again. I was scared I was going to lose you". She hugged me again and then we walked over to her Father and he said, "Welcome back Mya, I hope you are pleased to be back home, but those arrangements were necessary for your health and my daughter. You do understand?"

"Of course, Master I do understand, I would not like Miss Sarah to be ill. I hope I don't become so sick again Master, please forgive".

"Oh stop being silly child, it was not your fault. Now go and do what you girls do and we will talk another time. Go on now". He kissed Miss Sarah and then we walked to her room as if nothing had ever happened.

A few months went by and then it began again. He would call me. I would go and then I would fall pregnant again. Each time this happen my Mother tended to me and my babies were taken away. By the time I was seventeen I had four children which I never knew of and one was a girl. I was quite sadden by this and decided I was not going to have anymore.

I asked my Mother is she knew of any prevention to stop me from breeding she told me yes but that as long as I continued to have them massa would always treat me right. She began to be upset with me and then me with her. I could not or understand why she wants this for me. It was like she did not care about me. I felt alone.

Miss Sarah was growing up to be the most beautiful and sort after Lady. Her Father kept many balls, each one I was invited too, but if I received too much attention I would be dismissed and sent to my room, as I no longer slept in Miss Sarah's room.

That's when I realised, I looked different I could pass as one of their kind, white! One day came when Master had his full of me and giggling away I asked him a bit afraid, but asked anyway, "Master, Sir, what would happen to my Mother and me if anything happened to you?" He looked at me quite surprised and then said, "Why? Come here girl I have for a long time ago drawn up your papers of freedom. That little cottage and the land around it, belongs to you and your Mother. You are more than a daughter to me. I just wish you had come along when I was younger. I never used to be so fat and ugly. In fact all of the ladies wanted me, but after Sarah's mother died I promised I would never marry again. You are all I need now". He looked at me and then said,"Why do you ask?

I answered him back, "No reason, Master, just wanted to know, that's all. Soon Miss Sarah will get married and I was just wondering what would happen to me, that's all".

He pulled me on his lap, "Nothing, my darling Mya. Now I insist you take those thoughts out of your head and while we are at it do you have anything to ask of me and I will, I promise give it to you".

I thought clearly for a moment and in an instant I knew and then I said to him, "May I, please Master keep my next baby. He doesn't have to live here. He or she can live with my Mother, but more than anything else may I please keep my next baby?"

He looked at me and got up suddenly. I nearly fell to the floor. He rubbed his chin and then started to laugh. He bent forward and then said, "Yes, you may because you my Mya have given me great pleasure. So yes I will grant your wish and you will it only when I say so. I will also draw up its papers for freedom right now".

He looked up at me, hesitating as he held on to the pen and then nodding his head done exactly as he said. My baby would be free and so would my Mother and I as long as he lived.

He showed me the paper and then put it in our special box and then with his hand sent me away. As I ran up the back stairway I, for some reason I began to think of ways to get rid of Master. I felt horrible, but this was our chance for freedom. I was already with child again. I knew it and I had known for some time but did not tell anyone.

Sarah was already engaged by now and that was all she could or would talk about and taking me with her. I was leaving my Mother. I had to device a plan.

The only thing Master wanted from me was my body and children. I would give it to him gladly and more strenuous, he was old and with that kind of love making he would not last long.

I could not think of anything else, but time was not on my side. It was only a matter of month or two before they would send me away again. I had to do it quick. I felt sorry for Master in a way but I had to think of myself and my Mother. We had to get away before Sarah got married, before they moved my Mother and even me off this plantation after her marriage. That's all she kept talking about. The guilt fled in an instant as I thought about our future. My Mother was beginning to look old.

Master called again. I dressed in one of my finest gowns and applied some rose oil on my neck. If this did not work, then it I could think of nothing else. I went to him. He looked pleased and commented on my beauty and how good I smelt. He took me for what seemed hours and only stopped because he was panting and tired. He said to me, "Tonight Mya, you have pleased me so much, why?" I answered him back, "Because Master, you have pleased me so much I wanted to make you happy and show you how grateful I am for all that you have done. That is all. Did I displease you?"

"Oh know, quite the opposite". Then he took me again. The next day he called for me again. I did the same and went to him. I felt sorry for him in a way because if he knew of my intentions then I knew that would mean my death. Again he stopped, his breathing becoming slower and slower. I shoved him down and told him I would do it as I could still see he wanted me. By the time I had my way with him, he could hardly breathe.

He pushed me away and pulled the sash for the servants. I was gone before they came. The next day everyone in the household was running around in desperation, but what I could hear Master was very ill. A few days later he was dead.

Whilst everyone was busy dealing with the funeral arrangements I crept into his room and took out our special box. I opened it up slowly and there, Lord and behold was everything he promised. I took the box and put under my skirt and looking around to make sure no one saw me quickly made my way to my room.

I rang my bell of the maidservant Master had for my personal well being and gave her a note. It was for my Mother. It told her to be ready after funeral because we were leaving and for now that's all she needed to know. I wrote it in our language just in case in reached the wrong hands.

She came back to me forthwith and told me it was delivered and I could see that she was curious. I dismissed her and told her to heat up some water for my bath.

I went to see Miss Sarah as I knew this would be the last time I would see her. She was kind and loving towards me and I would never forget that and in my own way I loved her too and I hoped she would be happy would her husband.

We spoke for a little while and played and joked around. She tried on loads of her beautiful gowns and carried on like her Father had not died. She was happy. Who could blame. This was all hers now and despite what anyone thought of her she was a gentle person. They would be treated fairly especially if her husband was anything like her.

I watched her as she danced around her room and she still looked a little child. Untouched and quite vulnerable to what lay ahead of her, whereas I knew a lot more, even though she was older than me. I then got up off her bed and made up an excuse to leave. She laughed and kissed me and carried on dancing, without a care in the world.

I went back to my room and packed a few things. Some of my clothes I put on I did not want to cause suspicion by taking all of my clothes. I only took what I needed. Everything of real importance that I truly needed was in the box. We were free.

I could not wait to see Mother. I rang the sash again. She came quickly. Nosey. I told her to summon the carriage has I had to see my Mother urgently. She asked me if I needed assistance. I did not trust her. "Just do as I say and hurry along, otherwise I will tell the Mistress. You are mines are you not? Master, doing the sign of the cross, gave you to me. So do not question me. Just do as I tell you and hurry up".

She ran out of my room quietly closing it behind her and as she done so I got up and opened it and treading softly in the hallway I could hear her whispering to the other slaves. I screamed down at her, "Now you will get lashes for that and will watch before I depart".

I heard footsteps and then I heard her voice shouting for the carriage and for them to send message to my Mother of my arrival. For the first time in my life I felt like I had power and know I knew what slavery was all about. I was going to use it to my advantage, but at the same time I was not going to inflict it or punish any one of them for their ignorance. They had been punishing me all of life since I arrived on this plantation. I was not going to stoop to their level. In fact, quite the opposite, I was going to help them.

The carriage came and see picked up my little suitcase, which she had seen on many occasions. So this should not show anything abnormal to my behaviour besides the fact that it was normally the Master who made the arrangements.

She helped me aboard and stood there as we rode off.

When we arrived at Mother's I told her to get her things, as much as she could carry and all of her belongings behind the curtain. We were not coming back from the cottage. She hurried and the horseman helped her.

When we began to get closer I told she to get the slaves and she did and then I told them to ahead and retain another one and purchase it using Miss Sarah's name.

My Mother and I rode along to the cottage, but I told the horseman to stop and leave us at a reputable Inn and come back tomorrow when everything was prepared. He escorted us in and acquired the room. I thanked him and he tipped his hat and we walked up the stairs.

Once in the room I grabbed my Mother by the hands and told her everything. She began to cry. I held her in my arms and showed her the papers, telling her and proving to her we were free and that the baby I was carrying was free as well.

Master had it all written up before he died. The cottage, our servants all belonged to us and we would want for nothing again. She looked at me and then said, "Chile what have you done?"

I answered her, "What do you mean? "Nothing! He showed me the papers along time ago and said we would be free when he died. Well he is dead now and that is all that matters. I had play in the matter Mother. He was an old man. He was going to die sooner or later. I don't see Miss Sarah shedding no tears. She doesn't even know I have these papers and we are never to lose them. Do you understand me Mother? No man is going to take advantage of us again. We can be together now as you promised. You are carrying on like it is my entire fault. He is dead and that is that and we are free".

She shook her head. I took my gloves and hat off and kissed her and holding up her head, I said, "Mother we are FREE".

OPPRESSION TO PROGRESSION FOR BLACK WOMEN IN SLAVERY

By Sandra Maddix

DEDICATION

To all of the people who have inspired me throughout my life to eventually write this book that has been waiting a long time to be written by me, myself and I.

I would especially like to send out a special Thank you to a certain person who assisted me at TVU university as my Head Tutor and believed in me and also to all of my family and friends who have stood by me. Thank you all!

Sandra

INTRODUCTION

Firstly, before I begin my book I should inform that this book is based on fact and not fiction and that the period in slavery that I will be focusing upon will cover the period between the mid eighteenth century and the early twentieth century.

It will relate to White Europeans colonising the West Indian Islands and using Black people as a source of free labour.

I will be using the West Indian Islands as my main source of reference to illicit black women's experiences of slavery. However, it will be necessary to draw upon the historical references of Black women in America who rebelled against slavery and fought for the liberation of Black women even after the emancipation of slavery.

This action had to happen in order to illustrate/ demonstrate a Black woman's transition from oppression to progression in and from slavery to their fight for equality and freedom.

Throughout my book I will use references by others authors to confirm my findings and through my book I hope in successfully delivering an uncomplicated version of the occurrences of exactly what happened during this period of time of slavery.

It is quite a difficult subject to brooch and it can consume a person for all different kinds of reasons if looked at in if a subjective way and then again contrary to that, also in an objective way. You have to be objective to a certain extent and understand that during this time it was seen as 'normal', even if not seen as 'wrong or unjust'.

AND SO IT BEGINS

Slavery was a basically a condition of being in bondage with no legal rights. Black slaves especially were considered as chattel and completely at the mercy of their enslavers.

The European and American people who were the enslavers recognised that black people could be more readily identified because of their colour within the population and therefore the necessity for white indentured servants to be imported to the West Indian Islands and America for labour not so prevalent, as if they escaped they could easily blend in remain unidentifiable, unlike the black slaves.

Slavery of black people began in the European colonies before America. Both Beckles and Bush, explain how slavery occurred in the European colonies and the economical reasons behind its development.

As an overview slavery was diverse and severe and refers specifically to the experiences of black people's lives. There was a sequential development and longevity to slavery in which black people suffered and were denied any legal or moral rights.

A slave's period of servitude depended upon his/her racial lineage, personality and attitude and that of their current slave master. A slave was expected to be obedient and subservient in all aspects of a slave's life. They were not seen as people. If a slave was rebellious then the repercussions for their actions would be tremendously severe.

They would most definitely be punished or killed as an example to the other slaves. This was usually most effective in the beginning of slavery, but as time went by the slaves' attitude began to change quite significantly.

This form of punishment was used by the slave masters in order to make them realise that they were just slaves and subservient to their enslavers. The plantations owners were willing to go to any length to maintain order and because of this they felt it extremely necessary to use any form of punishment to ensure discipline amongst the slaves.

Slaves were not seen as people with feelings who could experience or learn from moderate forms of discipline and so in order to make them realise that they were just slaves and nothing else but slaves and subservient to their enslavers, the punishments they received were very harsh and sometimes resulted in death. The plantation owners were willing to go to any length and use severe forms of punishments of any nature to ensure discipline amongst the slaves and the effectiveness of this form of discipline, proved at first to be quite effective.

Black females in particular had to undergo the same disciplines and punishments as black male slaves. They were whipped and had to suffer solitary confinement without nourishment, basically nothing at all.

Black women suffered from additional layers of oppression, as well as being enslaved they had to endure sexism at the hands of their own black men and white patriarchism. My work shows how us how and why women suffered at the hands of their enslavers in such a way, it can only be described as inhumane.

White women's racism and prejudice accounted for additional oppressive experiences for black women in slavery. They were seen as menial, stupid, interfering animals and they detested them even the more if their husband's showed sexual interest. Jealousy, therefore, became another form of them unleashing punishment unto the female slaves.

It is in my opinion also as an historian to totally agree with the other historian that black female slaves did suffer more at the hands of their slave masters. The realities of slavery are disgusting and quite unbelievable but the harsh reality of it is they did encounter much more than their male counterpart.

All of my findings substantiates these findings and agrees that in my opinion with all the oppression from every race and gender in slavery, black female slaves did suffer extremely more during the West Indian slave trade.

If you think about it, black women, when it comes to slavery are only secondary in our minds. Because we think of them firstly as a woman and then a 'slave' . We refuse to believe that they could have been treated as the black male slave. But it is said that whilst institutionalised sexism was a social system that protected black males sexuality; but it socially legitimised sexual exploitation of black females.

I am not suggesting that any form of slavery is just. Slavery of any kind is still slavery, whether you worked in the fields or as a maid. A slave is still a slave!

INJUSTICES OF SLAVERY

Female slaves were considered to be subordinate to all men and suffered from sexual as well as physical harassment, racial discrimination and also victimisation.

They were thought of as expendable and less valuable in the economic market. They were cheaper to buy and therefore outnumbered the amount of black male slaves that worked in the fields and because of the mortality rate of a field labourer, which was that of only twenty years, females worked in the fields as it was less of a financial liability to use black males in the fields.

This should explain how black female slaves were used to work the sugar plantations instead of the black males because they were cheaper to buy and therefore the black male slaves were considered more valuable as possessions than the females.

Even within their own black slave communities, black female slaves had to endure and be subjected to their own black counterparts treating them as non-equals. Class exploitation existed from their own male counterparts as well as their slave masters.

When you take all of these factors into account you will realise that the black female slave had to overcome from more oppression, more injustices, sexism and racism, therefore her achievements were more substantial in comparison to that of the black male slave. (Bell Hooks p.45), quotes, Black women and men often performed the exact same tasks in agricultural labour, but even in that area black women could rise to leadership positions........'.

As well as working in the fields and in the house, female slaves were expected to perform sexual duties for their masters with the intent to 'breed' to increase his economical status and slave population, whether it be for keeping them for his own slaves or for sale.

Sexual relation between female slaves and their masters was generally accepted and recognised to be part of the social structure of the Islands. Sexual relationship between female slaves and slave masters was prevalent and not just a part of West Indian culture, but further, also of the slave culture in America.

Black female's slaves bred to provide and depending on gender, domestic slaves were considered to be more handsome and hygienic because of their congeniality, economics and social convenience. (Inkori & Engerman p.382) supports the fact that society did create the supposition that something changed could become something better.

The only problem with this theory and form of reasoning is that is did not actually take place amongst the African slaves but the American and West Indian slaves once race dilution occurred between master and slave.

When we look at social change and the French's ideology of improving the black race, we can observe why black female slaves were abused sexually as a product to interbreed and continuation of this form of breeding continuing further dilution until some black slaves could actually pass as white, but it did not change their status as a female slave and they were even further subjected to an even harsher hatred amongst their own kind and whites because of this!

This selective form of breeding shows us how women were exploited sexually and brought mainly if not for economical reasons but for breeding purposes. Also, the more they were diluted, the more economical value they would be in slavery. The more their white masters thought of them of being more hygienic and congenial.

Their lighter complexion made them economically and socially more upstanding for the master's social status in the community and amongst his peers. They were bred for not only convenience but also for the amount of influence their master could receive and his position in the infrastructure within his society.

Society did create the supposition that change and racial dilution would create a 'better' slave and one of more costly reward for the master. They actually took on this form of reasoning to make it effective, without consciousness and race dilution did in fact deem a necessity in order to entail the economical enterprise of the master and plantation.

This created another social structure entirely based on their breeding interaction and dilution factor. This also caused black male slaves to imitate the role of their slavemaster and abuse black female slaves even more harshly.

Black female slave were considered promiscuous and with the excuse of polygamy within the slave community, their masters felt justified to use female slaves to satisfy their sexual needs and financial gains.

Slave masters believed that female slaves had different aspiration, needs and functions and therefore created a concubine system to satisfy not only their needs but families within the white hierarchy to breed and satisfy their sexual needs.

A poem taken from Binder & Reimers p,47 ".....both just alike, except the white.....", suggests that slave owners found black female slaves much more satisfying than that of their own white women.

Even though saying the above, black female slaves still had to encounter all of the harsh conditions of slavery and they were not made exempt from any of the punishments incurred from being a breeder or elite slave. (Bell Hooks).

Some black female slaves if they did not conceive, then it could be punishable by death. But you still have to take into account that they were still expected to fulfil their duties in any form of work even whilst pregnant. If they refused, they were then flogged, kicked in the belly and hanged by their arms whilst being punished.

All the slaves would watch as they were being punished. Some believed she deserved it and some did not, but at this time of slavery any other thought was usually dismissed as it would mean they also would be punished or killed for retaliating. They were just slaves and nothing more, at the whim of their masters and that of the slave owner.

This selective form of breeding shows us women wee exploited sexually and brought mainly for breeding purposes and how social change created an elite social structure amongst the slaves, which created more discrimination and victimisation for black female slaves.

There are indications throughout slavery that black men instead of assuming a protective role of towards their black women. They actually imitated their slave masters and abused them even further. They believed them to be promiscuous and with that same excuse of polygamy they felt justified to use the female also to satisfy their own sexual needs.

The elite black female slave was not allowed to have sexual relations with black men and this did evidently produce selectivity which resulted in even more obverse racism towards black women in slavery from all of the other people on the plantation.

After 1807 provisions were made to exempt pregnant slaves from floggings. The first legislation that came about forbade the whipping of black women. This was introduced in Trinidad in 1823. The planters felt outraged by this because they believed that the women were insolvent and began to show more resistance than the male slaves and that the punishment if it may have seemed extreme was extremely necessary in order to maintain order on the plantations. Black female slaves were deemed more dangerous and should be punished accordingly despite their condition or sexuality.

Legislations throughout the British West Indian colonies during the 1820's did forbid the whipping of female slaves. Whilst men did receive whippings, women were punished by being kept in solitary confinement or 'stocks'. But these forms of punishments did nothing to deter them from rebelling and demanding better treatment because of their condition and sexuality.

Even Parliament, had their own agenda towards slavery. Today it would definitely be interpreted as a form of racism and sexism and the slave trade was promoted because of the economical factors and the plantation owners had little regard to what the abolitionists had to say to bring forward to the public's attention in regards to the inhumane injustices of slavery.

Even though in Jamaican laws of 1826, the flogging of a pregnant woman was recognised as inhumane and concessions were made, nothing changed. As late as 1883, black female slaves still continued to endure floggings. A particular woman, Germaine on the Baillies Bacolet plantation in Grenada, received fifteen lashes for destroying the cane fields and neglecting her duties. What actually became of her after this attack still remains a debatable issue between all historians.

OPPRESSION

There was a hierarchy in slavery and depending on where you were graded within that system, determined the way you were treated. Basically there were classified into their racial groups and these were Africans, creoles, maroons, mulattos, slaves with elitist status and freed men and women of colour. (Mathurin, 1975) informs us that a slave's racial lineage determined their very existence and how they would live through life.

The hierarchial slavery system was produced because of anthropometric assertions and social organisation which also produced group hierarchy. Women were used as "Breeders" to produce a variety of different types of workers and the reason why I say this is because no matter what your race dilution, you were still considered to be black and inferior to white people and therefore you still had to work. The only difference was the type of work you would have to do. Basically, black women produced, brown women served and white women consumed.

The racial and ethnic lines determined the value of the slaves and predicted the lifestyle they would lead and the type of work that they were destined to do. For instance, the slave elitists were mainly artisans and females they were not considered to be skilled workers and so did not benefit from this status.

Freed women were alienated from society and mulattos were deemed unable to toil the land and therefore the Africans had to do it. This increased the black male slaves to dislike the elitist slaves on the plantation, which would normally result in them being more intolerable of the black female slaves and treat them with even more indifference.

Plantations were still building weaning houses in Jamaica in order to get black women, freed or not back to work, even if it meant back into the fields where they felt like they still belonged.

As early as 1790, especially in Jamaica on the Worthy Park and Mesopotamia Plantations the ratio of women workers in the fields compared to that of their black male slaves was doubled or higher. This obviously shows you that black women were expendable even when used for economical gain.

On the Sarah Plantation in a six month period from January to June 1827, out of a total of 171 slaves, thirty four were punished and twenty one were women. This not only proves that women were subjected more harshly under slavery, but also that they were deemed more expendable.

Due to their behaviour, they were punished and sexuality abused by their masters and black male slaves. Victimisation increased and because of status and dilution they had reached a level of hierarchy within slavery which was not open to men, even then. They were still considered to be inferior in all categories.

Their own black man would whip them and abuse them because of their own position on the plantation. What most of them neglected to realise is that if it was not for the female slaves they would never had attained that position because of the degradation they were subjected to.

Female domestics suffered just as much, perhaps even more because not only did they have to obey their slave master who would inflict punishment unto them, but also that of the wife. This could be at times prove to be quite fatal and most of the times the reason behind it was purely jealously. This just proves that throughout slavery the black females were always treated the same and basically it never got any better, if not, worse.

REBELLION

From the time that the transatlantic slave trade began women were rebelling, even to the extreme point of taking their own lives in order not to becomes slaves. This would occur from once they were captured and loaded onto the ships. The abuse began from then.

On one such incident it is noted in Binder & Reimers that a slave on board a ship named Elizabeth was found hanged, dead in the morning with a rope tied around her neck.

The Atlantic slave trade had a preference for capturing women and children because they were easier to move. Women as well as being captured to be enslaved had to suffer all of the indignities that went along with slavery and again sexual harassment. They were regarded as fair prey for the sailors.

But saying all of the above women were the primary agents in the emancipation of slavery. They were resilient from the beginning until the end. They endured a pain and suffering that is unconceivable even in this time and many lost their lives in doing so.

They rebelled in a regime of enslavement that was unjust and in doing so underwent severe punishment, but knowing so, that one day emancipation would occur and they would be liberated.

Due to their continuous fight they eventually managed to unite and create a resistance against slavery bonding race and culture, which protected slaves from total exploitation and extinction and even though the slave masters tried to contest this on legislation/moral grounds and the value of black people some of them did not succeed.

An example of this is the Antebellum South which was owned by James Henry Hammond and when checking his records you will observe that his slaves were more independent and had more control on his plantations than his surrounding neighbours. You can imagine how his neighbours on the other plantations regarded this man and how they demonstrated their thoughts towards him in public. He must of felt inferior and belittled as a slave master and plantation owner. He, himself, was an outcast to society.

Tradition and community were more important to the slaves and the cohesive effect this had on them made them realise that it was far more important to remain together, unite as a people and become strong to lead a rebellion than to be an individualist.

Insubordination encouraged cultural and personal autonomy from the demands of the plantations and women expressed their cultural defiance when working in the fields through songs and language which they used as a defence mechanism against dehumanisation and this helped to maintain the general spirit in the resistance against slavery.

Women also rebelled by deliberately, physically assaulting white people to show other slaves that it could be done, even though they knew the consequences. This form of rebellion intimidated their slave masters or masters but made the women more confident in their resistance to slavery.

Many women rebelled even knowing the consequential punishments they could encounter. I will know continue to re-establish how they influenced the slave trade and I will leave it up to you to determine their fate as most of them were never recorded, but their records of what they accomplished should prove that no form of leniency was given and they were made example of what may come to others.

In Barbados in 1816, Nanny Griggs, a slave, was the ringleader in one of these revolts. She informed the slaves of oncoming freedom and when this did not happen and they were beginning to feel deflated she encouraged them to commit arson.

Now, no one can testify what actually happened to Nanny Griggs, but if she survived and by examination of certain records I reckon not, she definitely did cause a notice amongst the slaves and their masters.

Women and by now men became more defiant and adamant to resist and attempt to stand up to their masters.

Within the slave community, women, marketers and 'higglers' were seen as a threat to their masters because of their financial independence. The fact that they were self-reliant meant that they did not have to depend upon their black men and their independence did give them a way to attain freedom from the sexual harassment and slavery confinement of their white masters.

Women showed an overall pattern of continuous resistance and were the main offenders on the plantations, but they were still undermined and punished as such according to their influence and the effect of the crime. The punishments definitely became harsher and sometimes death was the only answer to warn the other slaves who may have the same ideas. Leadership from the slave masters had to become more effective as rebellion increased.

These independent women had a positive effect on the slaves and gave them hope in their rebellion because due to their trade they could be used as spies and messengers. Due to the fact they out amongst the general community gave them cause not to attract too much attention. Also the fact that being a slave they were not looked upon as have the intelligent to achieve but less enact such a force to be reckon with.

Also the European perception of women allowed the slave woman to get away with the same acts because of their same beliefs of their assumed illiteracy or educational factor that a slave could actually come to thought of such plans. They were thought of ignorant and incapable of learning and therefore, inadequate of having the ability to create a plan of any kind to enable rebellion, much less incitement, with the outlook of rebellion.

It was inconceivable to men that they could be seen as fighters or leaders, but women were the primary agents in the rebellion that finally led to the emancipation of slavery. They could not be intelligent enough and they definitely were not educated. It was unthinkable and therefore this would cause or contrive the thoughts of conspiracy amongst their own white people in aiding or abetting the blacks in their fight for freedom via rebellion.

Their continuous complaints and actions against slavery made Europeans eventually see the immortality of slavery, especially from a religious viewpoint and this did lead to slaves finally being emancipated, but not before all forms of rebellion had taken place, which of course took quite some time.

Some forms of rebellion were quite extreme, such as mutilation, so as not to enable them to work, which sometimes resulted in suicide. Women also poisoned their masters, but their general lack of gratitude and respect was their strongest form of revolt.

Escape was another form of rebellion. It depended on the help from other slaves and women. It was generally practiced in order to re-unite them with their missing partners or to find their children.

As women continued to rebel and emancipation did occur, women found that they still had to experience alienation, prejudice and discrimination. For a time it took them a lot longer to actually achieve recognition because of sexism and various legislations being passed which kept them in bondage and labelled them as inferior beings and people who could not be dependent. They were still deemed as 'nothing'.

A proclamation issued as memorandums by Lord Lugard on 22nd November 1901, recommended the 'Disposal of Liberated Women'. Quote........."pertaining to female slaves they were to be considered a subcategory of matrimony, which enabled the transfer and redemption of female slaves under the guise of marriage and classified the estrangement of masters and female slaves as divorce, unable to escape from slavery............" . (Inkori & Engerman p.56).

From the above quotation you can observe that this memorandum saw black women as inferior to black and white males. They did not acquire their freedom so easily and were still looked upon as burdensome and experienced inequity.

Even though slavery had ended it had not for women. Sexism and racism formed further segregation and ensured patriarchal control and rule. All of the memorandums issued at the time were unfair to women and allowed them no rights.

Memorandum no.32, recognised that women needed to be protected and that even though they were meant to be free in reality they were still slaves to society and men in the eyes of the law and everyone else.

PROGRESSION

Black women fought against slavery all around the world. They were involved in campaigns that bought recognition to the public to make them aware of the injustices of slavery. They were active in speaking about slavery and writing autobiographical novels accounting their experiences to show the world just how much they had suffered and were still suffering.

Women were pioneers in the crusades for women rights, which even after the emancipation of slavery still took along time being recognised for the cause of women's rights and that of the black women. They still through it all suffered and were subjected to racism, sexism and segregation. Still unrecognised by society at large.

Even white women who fought for the emancipation of slavery failed to recognised that black women existed and were fighting for their own emancipation from the male viewpoint, because if black males were liberated then they should gain liberation and equality in their own society, solely on the fact that they were white and above the black man, who by this time had more liberation than themselves.

White women fought for themselves and believed that they should receive the same legal recognition and equality. They won, but this constitution did not involve or include black women.

Sojourner Truth was born a slave in 1797 in New York and was legally emancipated in 1827 by that state. On her freedom she travelled east preaching about slavery and believed that she had more to offer than being a domestic servant to the white people. Her first book was published in 1850 and it was a narrative that told her story about slavery from a northern woman's perspective.

WOMEN WHO FOUGHT FOR LIBERATION AND THE EMANCIPATION OF SLAVERY

Sojourner Truth began to crusade for women rights and even though reluctant, white feminists included her in their convention at the Akron Woman's Right Convention, as a speaker, where she gave her famous speech of "Aren't I A Woman".

Her speech made people aware of the fact that women worked just as hard as the black male slaves and were treated equally in punishment, if not worse than their male counterparts in slavery and therefore should be regarded just as equally as men in a free society.

Mary Prince, obtained freedom once in Britain in 1828. She wrote an autobiographical account of her life as a slave and was the first woman to petition against slavery to the British Parliament. This was what a slave's life was really like and all of the injustices she had to endure as a slave.

Her only concern was for that of her family that was left behind and one day being reunited with them. Her story basically informs us of her resistance to slavery and what she had to forego in order to attain final freedom.

Anna Julia Cooper was born a slave in 1858 in North Carolina. She had the opportunity to be educated and graduated from college 1884. She became a teacher and believed in the liberation for all African-American men and women, but believed that this could only be achieved through education.

Anna Julia Cooper wrote a book that indicated to society that female issues had to be taken into account and was equal to that of male issues. She played an active role in the suffrage movement for African-American women and fought for the right to vote and believed that black men and women should unite in order to achieve equality and power.

Many black women clubs were established in the 1890's and when Cooper gave a speech at the Women's Congress in Chicago in 1893 for the needs and status of black women she was invited by the National Councils of Women to join their organisation.

She continued to crusade for African-American women's rights and equality and her belief in education, as a power source for progression. She died in Washington D, C. 1964.

Mary Church Terrell Was born on 23 September 1863 in Memphis, Tennessee. She spent most of her early years at schools and colleges, when she finally graduated in 1884 and then became a teacher at Wilberforce University in Ohio where she taught for two years. She then came to Europe and learned French, German and Italian.

Mary Church Terrell found Europe enlightening because she was not classified by her race. It was after her time in Europe that she returned back to America to marry her husband Robert that she encountered a different reception.

In 1892 she was elected president of the National Association of Coloured Women, which merged with the Coloured Women's League of Washington, an organisation that she also co-founded. She also became the first black woman in the country to be appointed to a school board and became a member of the District of Colombia Board of Education.

Mary Church Terrell dedicated her life to fighting politically for the improvement of women and her race despite her age. She died at 90 years of age on 24th July 1954.

Ellen Craft was born in 1826 in Clinton, Georgia, a slave. She was renowned for her escape and that of her husband in December in 1848, where she disguised herself as a male slave owner and escaped to Philadelphia and then moved onto Boston

The Fugitive Slave Law caused them to flee again and they moved to England in December in 1850. Although free, she was still considered inferior and if she wanted to remain, then as the law stood at that time she would then be become a fugitive and treated as such. She had no intention of being treated like a 'slave' again, so she was forced to move on again, but her fight did not stop there and if anything it made her more determine to go on fighting for liberation.

Ellen Craft's escape story was published in England in 1852 and it was titled 'Running a Thousand Miles For Freedom'. In 1968 she then returned to America with her family and after a few years opened up an industrial school for coloured children in Georgia. She died in 1897 and was recognised for an escape that most people would otherwise find quite impossible in slavery

CONCLUSION

During slavery women had to deal with racial conflicts sexual abuse, sexism and prejudice. Inferior status and work put women at the bottom of hierarchial slave system.

Female slaves were looked upon as temptresses who would submit to their master's sexual advances to live an easier slave life but in actual fact this was not the case because they had no choice and if they resisted their slave masters they would be punished or raped.

Female Slave received the same punishment as their male counterparts, but it is in my opinion that they were punished more severely and used as and example to other slaves. QUOTE, "... the ultimate pain of having one's child sold away was a primary threat practised by white women against their black slave woman...". (Gordon, p.27). The white woman liked to feel the power they had over them and hurt them in the only way a woman knew how, by ultimately taking their child away from them and selling it to another plantation so that she would never see her baby again.

Women were degraded and portrayed as inferior beings and this form of description justified to the slave master and society that the way women were treated was unquestionable as after all they were only slaves. They believed that women deserved to be exploited and abused sexually and physically because they were an expendable commodity within the slave trade.

Black women In effect as you can see did not adhere to his stereotype and if you think about concubinage, you will realise as I did that they only accepted their way of life or slavery to survive. Their survival was foremost and it actually put them in a position to cause revolts and this gave them strength and independence in their fight for emancipation of slavery.

Women retained their independence and cultural autonomy which helped slaves to survive the actual slave experience and regime. Despite all of the injustices that the oppression of black females in slavery encountered, you will realise that alongside the black male slaves and help, it made the rebellion much more effective. They were able to maintain their dignity and culture and some of the brutality and segregation lessened, especially with the black male slaves.

Women kept the cohesiveness within the slave family, maintaining slave solidarity and communal stability.

Their resistance was crucial to the survival of the black slaves and self and her persistence in causing insurrection within the community and her personal involvement in the revolts is what finally led to the emancipation of slavery.

The emancipation of slavery did not give women ultimate freedom. Legislations made sure that they were kept 'enslaved' one way or another and women still had to struggle and fight for many more years for liberation and equality.

Elizabeth Keckley, was born a slave in Virginia in 1818. Sold to another slave master in North Carolina where she suffered rape and had a son for her slave master. She was then sold again to St. Louis where she met her husband James Keckley who lied to her about being a free man. She then again felt betrayed.

She fought and paid for her freedom and that of her son and left her husband after eight years of marriage. These actions made her even more determine to fight for the injustices of slavery and equality for the black women. Believe it or not she was an accomplished tradeswoman in dressmaking and even made clothes for Mrs Lincoln who later employed her as her official dressmaker and maid.

Elizabeth was not quite happy with the situation and still was not satisfied about the way black women were looked upon. In 1862 she helped to found the Contraband Relief Association to assist former slaves who had come to Washington D.C. hoping for a better life.

After the President's assassination she wrote a book titled, 'Behind the Scenes', which indicated what her life was like at the White House. Her relationship with Mrs Lincoln obviously deteriorated and she went to live in a home for destitute women and their children, where she lived off her dead son's pension, who died in the civil war. Elizabeth died in 1907 of a stroke.

These are just some of the women who were committed to liberation and the emancipation of the black women.

Considering the time and that they made such a difference in society and because of them the changes that made a difference to a way of life for the black women; I would like to give out my undeniable respect to them all and to all of the black people out there all over the world.

We are still struggling and with tools and knowledge that these slaves did not have at their advantage. We truly wonder how they must have achieved it because if you look at today's society many of the same things they were fighting for, like equality for example, still does not exist globally today.

Up to this day we still see how slavery has impacted on people all over the world and how it has affected black people in general and how they treat their own people of colour, with that same, identical ignorant as that of the very slaves they descended from.

Racism and prejudice still exist and hierarchy is still very active particular for women, especially women of colour. Therefore, it is in my opinion that a lot of work still remains to be done to rectify our indifferences and insecurities in our communities and all around the world.

It pains me to observe that in reality nothing has really changed and people are still fighting and it as always is still for economical gain and power and recognition/ status from their peers.

They do not appear to care who has to suffer whilst they reach to acquire their goal and who they hurt whilst they acquire it.

I hope my book will aspire people to look at themselves and if you can tick everything that was extremely worrying about slavery off my list then you are truly a good person, if not and you do care, there is help for everyone who wants it. So please lets all make a difference, if not for ourselves then for our future, or children.

EQUALITY FOR ALL AND SUFFERING FOR NONE!!!That's my adage and contribution.

(Unfortunately no documents of pictures or illustrations were included, but can at your discretion be obtainable via any books listed throughout my book and the authors who I quoted my book. Thank you)

EQUALITY FOR ALL! WE ARE ALL ONE!! SX

I AM FREE! SX

THE AUTHOR SANDRA MADDIX:

Printed in the United States
By Bookmasters